BRAVE BUNNY

BRAVE BUNNY

RUTH LERCHER BORNSTEIN

Gibbs Smith, Publisher
Salt Lake City

07 06 05 04 03   5 4 3 2 1

Published by
Gibbs Smith, Publisher
P.O. Box 667
Layton, Utah 84041

Orders: (1-800) 748-5439
www.gibbs-smith.com

Edited by Jennifer Grillone
Printed and bound in Korea

Originally published as *Indian Bunny* by Golden Gate Junior Books in 1973.
ISBN 0-516-08723-1

Library of Congress Cataloging-in-Publication Data

Bornstein, Ruth.
Brave bunny / story and illustrations by Ruth Bornstein.—1st ed.
p. cm.
Summary: A bunny decides that it is time to go into the world to meet and learn from other animals, especially his friend Owl.
ISBN 1-58685-282-5
[1. Rabbits—Fiction. 2. Owls—Fiction. 3. Forest animals—Fiction.]
Title.
PZ7.B64848Br 2003
[E]—dc21
                                    2003004843

For Jacob, Gabriel, Joseph, Rebekah, Kalia, and Olivia

One day a bunny said,

Good-bye, I'm going out into the world.

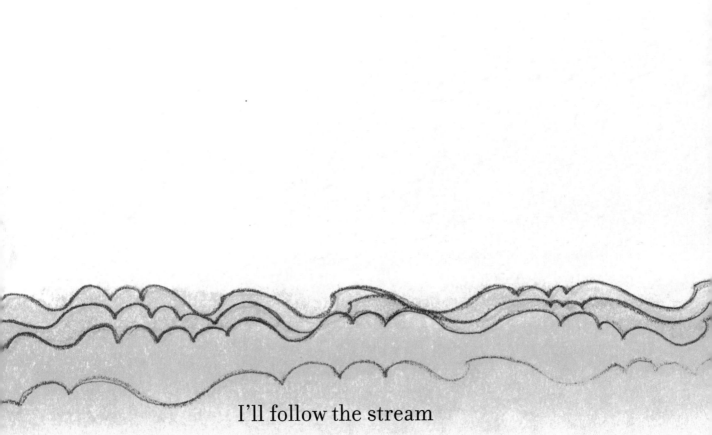

I'll follow the stream

And I'll walk along a hidden forest trail
                                    —so silently
that not even the deer will hear me.

In the stream I'll find a tadpole
and he'll tell me how he turns into a frog.

I'll come to a meadow
and do a deer dance when the sun is high.

I'll climb a tree
and look far out.

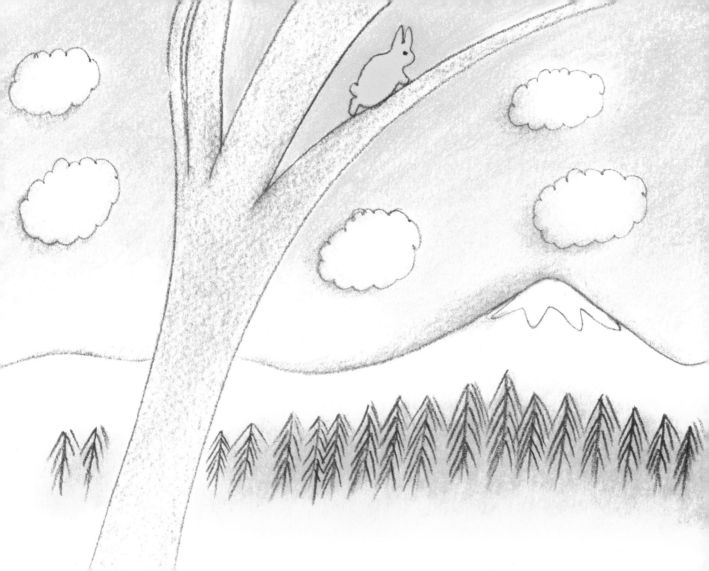

An eagle will come to his nest,
so I'll hide in my friend the Owl's house
and watch him.

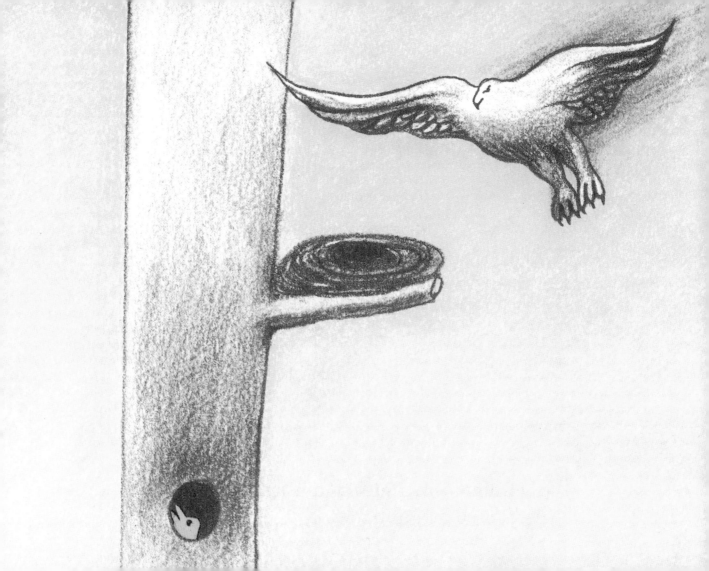

I'll climb down and find a feather the eagle
has floated down to me.

Then I'll follow the hidden trail

to the place where the animals meet.

And I'll watch them.

And when the sun is low

I'll silently steal away.

I'll gather round stones
to mark a place.

And I'll rub two sticks together
to make a fire.

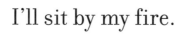

I'll sit by my fire.

Maybe I'll hear the drums far off . . .
faintly
faintly.

And I'll beat my drum in the night.

My friend the Owl will hear me.

And when the moon is high
and I crawl into my tepee,
my friend will fly over to say,

Good night, Brave Bunny.

Sweet dreams.